AFRICAN ANIMALS ABC

PHILIPPA-ALYS BROWNE

Barefoot Books
step inside a story

Antbear naps

Bushbaby blinks

Crocodile snaps

Dassie drinks

Elephant lumbers

Frog leaps

Giraffe dozes

Hippo sleeps

Impala grazes

Jackal prowls

Kingfisher dives

Lion growls

Monkey chatters

Nyala shivers

Ostrich dances

Porcupine quivers

Quail scuttles

Rhino stomps

Secretary bird stretches

Tortoise chomps

Umhutu hums

Vulture mutters

Warthog charges

Xoona moth flutters

Yellow-billed kite soars in the sky

Zebra watches the world go by

African Animal Facts

Antbear

This nocturnal mammal makes its home throughout Africa, south of the Sahara. The antbear lives alone, and during the day it can be found sleeping in its burrow in the ground. It eats mainly ants and termites.

Bushbaby

The thick-tailed bushbaby lives in east and southern Africa. Bushbaby habitats include woodlands, plantations and forests. Bushbabies eat fruit, seeds, leaves and insects.

Crocodile

The crocodile is a reptile that lives in warmer parts of Africa, Asia, Australia and America. Crocodiles warm up by basking in the sun all day. They go into the water at midday, when the ground is too hot for them, and in the evening. They eat almost anything – from weeds to insects, fish and even other crocodiles!

Dassie

Although the dassie is only the size of a rabbit, it is considered to be the nearest relative to the elephant! Dassies can be found all over Africa living in rocky hills and boulders. They eat a mainly vegetarian diet, ranging from fruit to tree bark and twigs.

Elephant

Elephants are mammals and are the largest living land animal. The African elephant is much bigger and wilder than the Indian elephant. It can be found all over Africa south of the Sahara. Elephants like to eat bark, pods, leaves and fruit.

Frog

Tree frogs can be found throughout Africa. Like all frogs, they are amphibians, which means they can live on land and in water. They mainly live in trees but a few live in water and some burrow in the ground.

Giraffe

Giraffes can be found in southern Africa up to Sudan and Ethiopia, and west to Senegal. These tall mammals eat shoots and twigs, but they like grasses too.

Hippopotamus

The hippopotamus is a mammal, distantly related to the pig. Hippos can be found throughout Africa in or by large rivers or swampy areas. During the day they sleep partially submerged with their heads and backs sticking out of the water.

Impala

Impala are a type of antelope that can be found grazing throughout the savannahs of southern Africa up to Kenya and Uganda, and across to Namibia and Angola. When scared or startled, impala snort and dash off with their tails raised in the air like white flags.

Jackal

The jackal is a fox-like creature. The black-backed jackal can be found in many areas of Africa, in woodlands or on the open plain. The jackal's diet ranges from fruit to rats, mice, reptiles and birds.

Kingfisher

Kingfishers are short-legged birds with dagger-like bills. They live in many parts of the world. The giant kingfisher can be found in all areas of Africa south of the Sahara, except the dry western parts. These birds live near wooded streams, dams and coastal lagoons, since their main food is fish.

Lion

Lions live all over Africa. These large cats live in all types of countryside except forests. They hunt both day and night, usually seeking mammals as their prey.

Monkey

The vervet monkey is found all over Africa. These creatures live in groups of up to twenty, in woodlands, savannahs and forests. They eat fruit, berries, leaves and roots.

Nyala

Nyala are a type of antelope that can be found in southern Africa. They live and graze in forests, and when they are scared, they make a barking sound!

Ostrich

This bird lives in isolated pockets throughout southern Africa. Ostriches cannot fly, but they can run extremely fast – up to 37 miles/60 kilometres per hour! When a male ostrich is excited, it often throws its throat into the air to make a lion-like roar.

Porcupine

The southern-African crested porcupine can be found everywhere from South Africa to Tanzania. Porcupines make a grunting, snuffling noise like a pig. They spend their time in caves or holes.

Quail

There are nearly 100 species of quail in the world. The harlequin quail can be found in pairs, and they live all over Africa. Quail eat mainly seeds, shoots and insects.

Rhinoceros

White and black rhinos, once found all over Africa, are now confined to highly protected areas south of the Sahara. They live among dense and thorny bushes. Rhinos have poor eyesight but a keen sense of smell, and communicate with each other by grunting, snorting and squealing.

Secretary Bird

These large birds live in pairs and can be seen walking through grassland areas south of the Sahara. Secretary birds eat insects, snakes, tortoises, young birds and other small animals.

Tortoise

This hard-shelled reptile can survive in a variety of habitats, from the desert to the forest. Tortoises can be found in central and eastern regions of South Africa, as well as Mozambique, Zimbabwe and northern Botswana. Their shells provide great protection as well as good camouflage.

Umhutu

The umhutu, or mosquito, is an insect. The common household mosquito can be found throughout Africa.

Vulture

The vulture lives throughout the area north of South Africa, up to Cairo and across to west Africa. Vultures are scavengers; they feed on the flesh of dead animals and spend much of their day soaring in the sky searching for food.

Warthog

This pig-like creature is widespread in Africa, and is usually to be seen in grasslands where there are trees and bushes to give cover. During the heat of the day, warthogs often take naps. In the cool of the evening, they look for roots and fruit to eat.

Xoona Moth

A moth is a flying insect that is active mainly at night. The cream-striped owl moth is common throughout Africa south of the Sahara. It is attracted to rotting fruit and sweet foods and drinks. This moth lays thousands of eggs, which hatch into larvae that eat acacia leaves.

Yellow-billed Kite

Kites are large, long-winged birds of prey with V-shaped tails. This bird is found all over Africa and spends most of the day flying low, looking for prey. The kite's nest consists of sticks laid in a tree.

Zebra

All species of this small, horse-like animal can be found in Africa. Zebras are generally seen in grasslands, roaming in large herds. They neigh like horses but make a high-pitched bark or squeal when fighting.

To Rosie and my other African mothers
— Philippa-Alys Browne

Barefoot Books
2067 Massachusetts Ave
Cambridge, MA 02140

Barefoot Books
294 Banbury Road
Oxford, OX2 7ED

Text copyright © 1995 by Stella Blackstone
Illustrations copyright © 1995 by Philippa-Alys Browne
The moral rights of Stella Blackstone and Philippa-Alys Browne have been asserted

First published in Great Britain by Barefoot Books, Ltd in 1995
and in the United States of America by Barefoot Books, Inc in 1998
This paperback edition first published in 2012
All rights reserved

Reproduction by B & P International, Hong Kong
Printed in China on 100% acid-free paper
This book was typeset in Flareserif, Gill Sans and Lithos

Paperback ISBN 978-1-84148-319-1
Board Book ISBN 978-1-84686-361-5

British Cataloguing-in-Publication Data:
a catalogue record for this book is available from the British Library

Library of Congress Cataloging-in-Publication Data is available under
LCCN 2008271197

1 3 5 7 9 8 6 4 2